THIS
BOOK
BELONGS
TO:

ALBION

Name: _____ Age: _____

Favourite player: _____

2023/24

My Predictions	Actual

The Seagulls' final position:

The Seagulls' top scorer:

Premier League winners:

Premier League top scorer:

FA Cup winners:

EFL Cup winners:

Contributors: Andy Greeves, Will Miller, Peter Rogers.

A TWOCAN PUBLICATION

978-1-915571-51-9

£11

CONTENTS

THE PREMIER LEAGUE
SQUAD
2023/24

Bart
VERBRUGGEN

1

POSITION: Goalkeeper   **COUNTRY:** Netherlands   **DOB:** 18/08/2002

Bart Verbruggen is a new signing for the club, joining after an impressive breakout season with Anderlecht, in which they reached the quarter-final of the UEFA Europa Conference League and he was chosen as their Player of the Season.

He is the epitome of the modern goalkeeper, just as confident with the ball at his feet as he is with it in his hands, which is vital to Brighton's ingrained style of play. He's also already carved out a reputation as a strong penalty saver.

Tariq
LAMPTEY

2

POSITION: **Defender**   COUNTRY: **Ghana**   DOB: **30/09/2000**

Tariq signed from Chelsea in 2020 in order to showcase his talents and did not take long to do so, emerging as one of the most dangerous attacking right-backs in the Premier League within the year. Assists flowed, as did praise for his unique zig-zag dribbling style.

Injuries curtailed that momentum, but Lamptey got back to full fitness this pre-season and will prove important again this term as Brighton battle on all fronts.

Igor
JULIO

3

POSITION: **Defender**   COUNTRY: **Brazil**   DOB: **07/02/1998**

A great way of preparing for a European campaign is to sign players with European experience. Step forward Igor Julio, who went all the way to the UEFA Europa Conference League final in 2023 with Fiorentina.

He's an uncompromising, tough-tackling centre-back with a good left foot, happy to drive forward with the ball or connect with his midfielders. After battling with the best Italy has to offer over the last three years, he'll now take the next step in the Premier League.

Adam
WEBSTER
4

POSITION: **Defender**   COUNTRY: **England**   DOB: **04/01/1995**

Adam Webster's been a consistent, reliable figure at the back for Brighton since joining the club in 2019.

Signed off the back of a Player of the Season campaign with Bristol City, a move to the Seagulls brought great expectations - but there's no doubt he has delivered on those.

He has continually fought off competition for the right to partner captain Lewis Dunk in the heart of defence, proving particularly strong in the passing game, which is key to Brighton's style.

Lewis
DUNK
5

POSITION: **Defender**   COUNTRY: **England**   DOB: **21/11/1991**

Club captain Lewis Dunk is entering his 15th season with the Seagulls, clocking up over 400 appearances in blue and white as the club has risen from League One to the UEFA Europa League.

He has been there every step of the way, adapting and improving continually on the journey upwards, leading from the back vocally and setting fresh, new standards for others to reach, whilst also providing the fans with a direct connection to the club.

His fine form has seen him return to the England fold in 2023 with a superb display in the 3-1 win against Scotland in September.

SQUAD
2023/24

James
MILNER

6

POSITION: Midfielder   **COUNTRY:** England   **DOB:** 04/01/1986

Brighton represents the next stop in James Milner's incredible, illustrious career, which has now entered its third decade at the top level. He is one of the modern game's true physical marvels.

He brings Champions League and Premier League-winning experience to a young squad, plus a positional versatility that will see him perform both in midfield and at full-back.

He will have plenty of influence - both on and off the pitch - for the Seagulls this campaign.

Solly MARCH — 7

POSITION: Midfielder **COUNTRY:** England **DOB:** 20/07/1994

The evolution of Solly March's game has been incredible.

He has played full-back, wing-back, wide midfielder all en route to becoming the fully-fledged, goalscoring winger he is today. Add to this the fact he hails from Sussex and emerged from the development squad, it's no wonder he's a fans' favourite.

Last season he scored seven times - his best-ever league tally - and this term he begun with three goals in three games. He was always a willing worker and teammate; now he's a true difference-maker too.

Mahmoud DAHOUD — 8

POSITION: Midfielder **COUNTRY:** Germany **DOB:** 01/01/1996

Mahmoud Dahoud joined Brighton on a free transfer over the summer from Borussia Dortmund, ringing in a fresh chapter in England after nine seasons in the German Bundesliga.

His game has changed over the years, starting out as an extremely dynamic, explosive midfielder, but then refining the edges in order to become a standout possession-based footballer.

That should suit Roberto De Zerbi's intentions brilliantly; expect Dahoud to be at the heart of plenty of dominant, pass-happy Brighton performances this season.

João
PEDRO

9

POSITION: Midfielder   **COUNTRY:** Brazil   **DOB:** 26/09/2001

João Pedro is back in the Premier League with Brighton after signing from Championship club Watford.

The Amex represents a fresh start for him, a chance for him to show the world the truly special things he can do with the ball. His mazy dribbling and clever movements made him a standout performer in the second tier last season; now, Roberto De Zerbi will look to harness that in a Brighton shirt.

He's already off the mark for his new club, netting on the opening day against Luton Town.

Julio
ENCISO

10

POSITION: Forward   **COUNTRY:** Paraguay   **DOB:** 23/01/2004

Julio Enciso enjoyed a stunning debut season with Brighton, scoring four goals and assisting two in just over 800 minutes, as Roberto De Zerbi integrated him into the first team during the second half of the season.

One of those goals - a long-range bullet against Manchester City - was so good, it was voted as Premier League Goal of the Season. It was the strike that held the champions to a draw and secured the point that confirmed the Seagulls' Europa League berth for 2023/24.

He is regarded as one of the league's brightest young talents.

Billy GILMOUR — 11

POSITION: Midfielder   **COUNTRY: Scotland**   **DOB: 11/06/2001**

When Billy Gilmour joined Brighton in 2022, it felt like a match made in heaven. The Scot emerged from Chelsea's academy as a brilliant ball-playing midfielder - having been coveted by Barcelona in the past - so the Seagulls' style naturally suited him.

His poise on the ball under pressure allows him to carry out Robert De Zerbi's wishes, controlling the tempo of games and linking play in the centre. He will continue to go from strength to strength in 2023/24.

Pascal GROSS — 13

POSITION: Midfielder   **COUNTRY: Germany**   **DOB: 15/06/1991**

Talk about making a statement: Pascal Gross was the first player through the door upon Brighton's promotion to the Premier League in 2017, and he has been nothing short of superb - in a variety of roles - in the six years since.

He is a true creative hub for the club, be it from open play or dead-ball situations, and has also shown incredible positional intelligence and versatility. His consistent performances have been rewarded with a call-up to the Germany squad in 2023, making his debut against Japan in September.

SQUAD
2023/24

Adam
LALLANA

14

POSITION: Midfielder   **COUNTRY:** England   **DOB:** 10/05/1988

Adam Lallana is proof that Brighton have always understood how to build a well-balanced squad. His experience in the game and leadership capabilities have been just as valuable off the pitch as his neat footwork and dribbling skills have been on it.

The creative midfielder captained Southampton up the divisions, moved to Liverpool and won the lot, and now he's guiding the Seagulls' younger generation while still playing an important role in Roberto De Zerbi's rotation.

Jakub
MODER

15

POSITION: Midfielder   **COUNTRY:** Poland   **DOB:** 07/04/1999

Jakub Moder missed the entire 2022/23 due to injury, but this season will be looking to fight for a role under manager Roberto De Zerbi. At his best, he is a powerful, ball-carrying midfielder whose cleverness also sees him take up good positions in the attacking third.

Moder also has some UEFA Europa League experience courtesy of his time with former club Lech Poznań, and has won 20 caps for Poland, scoring twice.

Danny
WELBECK

18

POSITION: Forward   **COUNTRY:** England   **DOB:** 26/11/1990

Danny Welbeck has proved an inspired signing for Brighton, having joined on a free transfer from Watford in the summer of 2020.

Injuries had restricted his influence on the game in the years before, but he's found a rhythm with the Seagulls and has repaid the club's faith with a steady goalscoring return and an all-round positive presence up front.

Meanwhile the guidance and advice he is able to offer young stars like Evan Ferguson is no doubt extremely valuable.

Carlos BALEBA 20

POSITION: Midfielder   **COUNTRY:** Cameroon   **DOB:** 04/01/2004

Carlos Baleba's star in football is rising fast. Just 18 months ago he moved to Europe with Lille, and after breaking into the first team in 2023, Brighton worked fast to secure his signature this summer.

The Cameroonian is full of energy on the pitch, able to play at breakneck pace and press opponents constantly. Those athletic qualities, combined with his ability to receive, turn and fire forward create the perfect combination for a box-to-box midfield player.

At 19 he's still learning, still developing, but is still capable of making an impact from the very beginning.

Kaoru MITOMA 22

POSITION: Midfielder   **COUNTRY:** Japan   **DOB:** 20/05/1997

It's no surprise Kaoru Mitoma has developed into one of the world's best dribblers - he wrote a thesis on the art of it at university! That research has paid off; he's a fearsome sight with the ball at his feet.

He has hit top form already this season, assisting against Luton Town, then scoring and assisting against Wolves, as Brighton started as they mean to carry on. He is blazing fast and incredibly nimble when ducking between challenges. Now he has added goals to his dribbles, he is one of the Premier League's most devastating wingers.

SQUAD
2023/24

Jason STEELE — 23

POSITION: Goalkeeper   **COUNTRY:** England   **DOB:** 18/08/1990

Good things come to those who wait. After four-and-a-half seasons of biding his time, training hard and improving his game, Jason Steele was finally given the chance to shine between the sticks in the Premier League for Brighton - and it's fair to say he took it.

His ability to play slick, accurate passes even while under pressure, which suits the Seagulls' overall tactical style of inviting pressure in order to play through it, has cemented his status. In fact, since 2010, Steele has registered an incredible seven assists. He was ahead of his time.

Simon ADINGRA — 24

POSITION: Forward   **COUNTRY:** Ivory Coast   **DOB:** 01/01/2002

Simon Adingra is a new face on the south coast, as although he signed over a year ago, he took in a loan year at Union Saint-Gilloise in 2022/23 in order to prepare for life in the Premier League.

The early signs, both from pre-season and Brighton's first league fixtures, are that he is now up to the task. He's an explosive presence with or without the ball and his finishing technique has been innovative, already providing some extremely exciting moments for the fans.

SQUAD
2023/24

Evan
FERGUSON
28

POSITION: Forward   **COUNTRY:** Republic of Ireland   **DOB:** 19/10/2004

2023/24 could be the year Evan Ferguson rises to the top. He is just 18 years of age and Roberto De Zerbi has tried to manage his early minutes as well as possible, but the talent is bursting at the seams.

An incredibly intelligent, yet also physical and robust striker, he's holding defenders off with his frame, then playing perfect passes - or hitting perfect strikes - with his feet. His ability to link with the midfield smartly, at times using just a single touch, hints at a player who's been at the top level for ten years, not just one! Those qualities were illustrated perfectly by his early-season hat-trick as the Seagulls defeated Newcastle 3-1 on home soil.

Jan Paul
VAN HECKE
29

POSITION: Defender   **COUNTRY:** Netherlands   **DOB:** 08/06/2000

Jan Paul van Hecke's adaptation to English football has been seamless. A Player of the Season-calibre loan campaign at Blackburn Rovers in 2021/22 opened up an opportunity to play first-team football at Brighton last year - an opportunity he seized with both hands.

Back in May he delivered his greatest-ever performance, keeping Golden Boot winner Erling Haaland quiet during a 1-1 draw with champions Manchester City. He has continued his progression into the 2023/24 campaign, featuring on a number of occasions.

Pervis
ESTUPIÑÁN
30

POSITION: Defender   **COUNTRY:** Ecuador   **DOB:** 21/01/1998

Even after just one season in the Premier League, the sight of Pervis Estupiñán flying up and down the left flank has become semi-iconic.

There's an endless energy to his game which carries him into the box in order to deliver goals and assists - then back the other way to help defend and regain the ball. Underlining it all is a natural speed that most cannot cope with.

It's no wonder he took to the league so easily and quickly - he's an experienced Ecuador international and has played in a Champions League semi-final with Villarreal.

Ansu
FATI
31

POSITION: Forward   **COUNTRY:** Spain   **DOB:** 31/10/2002

For years at Barcelona, there was a simple, yet comprehensive litmus test of a player: if Lionel Messi connects with you on the pitch, it's a hint that you're very, very good.

Messi's connection with Ansu Fati was immediate, and at age 16 he was already ripping through defences. Only injury setbacks on Fati's side prevented the partnership blossoming into something fierce.

With those injuries now behind him, Fati saw Brighton and Roberto De Zerbi as the perfect combination to get him back to his best. Fans will enjoy his clever movements, incredible speed and instinctive, unerring finishing.

Joël
VELTMAN
34

POSITION: Defender   **COUNTRY:** Netherlands   **DOB:** 15/01/1992

Signing Ajax academy graduates is typically a very reliable transfer strategy, and since joining in 2020, Joël Veltman has been a very reliable presence for Brighton.

He has been able to step in at right-back or centre-back, play in a back four or a back three, from a starting role or as a steadying substitute. Whatever the occasion or situation, whatever the need, Veltman's been there to help.

He signed a new contract in July, pledging two more years in blue and white.

Tom McGILL 38

POSITION: Goalkeeper   **COUNTRY:** Canada   **DOB:** 25/03/2000

Summer 2023 was seismic for Tom McGill. He signed a contract extension with Brighton to remain at the club he joined aged 14, then he made the CONCACAF Gold Cup Canada squad, taking in valuable tournament and international experience.

He'll put that to good use and continue learning from two super goalkeepers in Jason Steele and Bart Verbruggen back at Brighton, no doubt ready to step forward and play a greater role if the need arises.

Facundo BUONANOTTE 40

POSITION: Midfielder   **COUNTRY:** Argentina   **DOB:** 23/12/2004

Facundo Buonanotte arrived at Brighton from Argentine side Rosario Central in January and, like so many before him, settled into life on the south coast immediately.

He notched his first assist for the club in March against West Ham, then scored his first goal against Nottingham Forest in April. He has a lovely way of speeding up play and injecting excitement into attacking moves.

He has already made his senior debut for Argentina and will continue to blossom and grow in 2023/24.

BRIGHTON & HOVE ALBION

ONE OF THE HARDEST THINGS TO DO IN FOOTBALL IS TO STICK THE BALL IN THE BACK OF THE NET.

NOT LEAST BECAUSE THERE ARE USUALLY ELEVEN OTHER PLAYERS TRYING TO STOP YOU DOING JUST THAT!

SHOOTING
FROM
DISTANCE

Good service is obviously important, and a good understanding with your striking partner is also vital, but when it comes to spectacular strikes, practice is the key to hitting a consistently accurate and powerful shot and to developing the timing and power required.

EXERCISE

A small-sided pitch is set up with two 18-yard boxes put together, but the corners of the pitch are cut off as shown in the diagram. There are five players per team, including goalkeepers, but only one player is allowed in the opponent's half.

The aim of the drill is to work a shooting opportunity when you have the ball, with the likely chance being to shoot from outside your opponent's penalty area, from distance. The teams take it in turns to release the ball into play from their own 'keeper - usually by rolling out to an unmarked player.

18 YDS

SOCCER
SKILLS

KEY FACTORS

1. Attitude to shooting - be positive, have a go!
2. Technique - use laces, hit through the ball.
3. Do not sacrifice accuracy for power.
4. Wide angle shooting - aim for the far post.
5. Always follow up for rebounds!

The size of the pitch can be reduced for younger players, and it should be noted that these junior players should also be practicing with a size 4 or even a size 3 ball, depending on their age.

MAHMOUD
DAHOUD

ALBION WOMEN

JULIA ZIGIOTTI

Phillips' first game in charge was a narrow 3-2 defeat to Manchester United in their FA Cup semi-final on Saturday April 15, 2023. En route to the final four, Brighton thrashed West Bromwich Albion 7-0 in round four, put five past Coventry with no reply in the fifth round and kept another clean sheet in a 2-0 quarter-final victory over Birmingham City.

WSL highlights included edging a nine-goal thriller away at West Ham United before beating them on home soil too, and there were also wins over Reading (2-1), in front of 5,220 fans at the Amex, and against Everton (3-2). Danielle Carter finished as top scorer for 2022/23 with nine goals in all competitions.

Katie Robinson was named the Player of the Season and Young Player of the Season for 2022/23 while she also collected the Goal of the Season award for her audacious lob in the 3-2 win over Everton in April 2023. Julia Zigiotti was named the Players' Player of the 2022/23 campaign.

The 2022/23 campaign was Brighton & Hove Albion Women's fifth season in the FA Women's Super League (WSL).

They finished 11th in the table to secure their top-flight status after a rollercoaster campaign which saw them go on an impressive run to the semi-final of the Women's FA Cup, but also sat at the foot of the league with just a handful of games to go, as no less than four different managers took charge of the team during the season.

Hope Powell stepped down in October 2022 after five years at the helm with assistant manager Amy Merricks filling in until Jens Scheuer's appointment at the end of December. The former Bayern Munich Women manager left by mutual consent just 65 days later with Merricks reappointed interim boss until Melissa Phillips was given the head coach role on a two-year contract on April 7, 2023.

The American had started the campaign at London City Lionesses before moving to Angel City in California and then back to the UK, and Brighton.

KATIE ROBINSON

GOAL OF THE SEASON V EVERTON

DAZZLING
DEFENDERS

ADAM VIRGO, GORDON GREER AND SHANE DUFFY WERE ALL SUPERB SEAGULLS DEFENDERS, AND CONTINUING THAT TRADITION IS CURRENT HOME-GROWN HERO LEWIS DUNK.

Gordon Greer proved to be an inspired signing by then-Brighton boss Gus Poyet in August 2010 when the experienced central defender joined Albion in a £250,000 switch from League One rivals Swindon Town.

A fully committed defender, Greer brought a steely determination to the heart of the Albion rearguard. His leadership qualities saw him instantly installed as captain by Poyet and the player returned his manager's faith in him by leading the team to the 2010/11 League One title in his debut season with the Seagulls.

As part of a group of players to have represented the club at both Withdean Stadium and the Amex, Greer played a key role as Brighton established themselves as a force at Championship level. His form with Albion was rewarded in 2013 with the first of 11 international caps for Scotland.

Adam Virgo played over 150 games for the Seagulls over two separate spells with his hometown club.

Virgo is famously remembered for his dramatic late equaliser against Swindon Town in the 2004 Second Division Play-Off semi-final. After that memorable goal, he was part of the team that sealed promotion to the Championship with a 1-0 victory over Bristol City at the Millennium Stadium. He further enhanced his status at the club with eight goals as he helped Albion secure second tier status in 2004/05.

His outstanding performances for Albion earned him a big-money move to Scottish giants Celtic in 2005 before returning to Brighton in 2008.

ADAM VIRGO

DATE OF BIRTH:	25 January 1983
PLACE OF BIRTH:	Brighton
NATIONALITY:	English
ALBION APPEARANCES:	158
ALBION GOALS:	17
ALBION DEBUT:	9 January 2001
Brighton & Hove Albion 2 Brentford 2 (Football League Trophy)	

GORDON GREER

DATE OF BIRTH:	14 December 1980
PLACE OF BIRTH:	Glasgow
NATIONALITY:	Scottish
ALBION APPEARANCES:	234
ALBION GOALS:	5
ALBION DEBUT:	14 August 2010
Brighton & Hove Albion 2 Rochdale 2 (League One)	

Shane Duffy had a dream debut season with Brighton & Hove Albion in 2016/17 as the club secured the runners-up spot in the Championship and promotion to the Premier League.

Forming a solid partnership alongside Lewis Dunk at the heart of the Albion defence, Duffy then played a vital role in the Seagulls securing their top-flight status and establishing themselves in the Premier League.

Signed from Blackburn Rovers, Albion certainly benefitted from Duffy's commitment and consistency throughout his Amex career. A regular face in the Republic of Ireland team too, he remains Albion's most capped international.

SHANE DUFFY

DATE OF BIRTH:	1 January 1992
PLACE OF BIRTH:	Derry
NATIONALITY:	Irish
ALBION APPEARANCES:	150
ALBION GOALS:	9
ALBION DEBUT:	27 August 2016

Newcastle United 2 Brighton & Hove Albion 0 (Championship)

LEWIS DUNK

DATE OF BIRTH:	21 November 1991
PLACE OF BIRTH:	Brighton
NATIONALITY:	English
ALBION APPEARANCES:	419*
ALBION GOALS:	27*
ALBION DEBUT:	1 May 2010

MK Dons 0 Brighton & Hove Albion 0 (League One)

*AS AT THE END OF THE 2022/23 SEASON

Lewis Dunk provides a commanding presence at the heart of the Seagulls' defence with the Brighton-born defender having played a colossal part in the club's journey from League One to the Premier League.

A proud captain of his hometown club, Dunk has now made over 400 first-team appearances. His outstanding form at club level in 2022/23 won a recall to the England squad, and he was rewarded with his second cap in the Three Lions' 3-1 victory over Scotland at Hampden Park in September.

Having skippered the club to their highest league finish last season, the 31-year-old agreed a new contract in the summer of 2023 which sees him commit his future to the Seagulls through until June 2026.

SIMON
ADINGRA

24

FOOTY PHRASES

ALL OF THESE FOOTY PHRASES ARE HIDDEN IN THE GRID, EXCEPT FOR ONE ...BUT CAN YOU WORK OUT WHICH ONE? ANSWERS ON PAGE 62

BRIGHTON & HOVE ALBION

```
C A E S W Y V Y B H U G N U R Y M M U D
V U Q I D E R B Y D A Y O L U R T S S U
K F A D J L G T X T F C B E I A K C F P
I B H E O T L P Z R V N M W O J I R Y A
C M O F F S I D E R U L E E D S P E Y H
M E R U E I J R D E D A Q G S H L A X C
R X E R N H A T T R I C K O I L A M R T
E I Y O W W S L S N O W R S O Z Y E Y A
D C A A Z L W S J K T K Y V K B M R T M
A A L P X A U Y H M I D F I E D A R O E
E N P T K N F W G C P L J K A M K N L H
H W E J A I L O K H A O F O H I E C G T
G A M E O F T W O H A L V E S T R N U F
N V A I A H E S L F J D U A O I U O T O
I E G B I C L A S S A C T U P F G E V N
V D G O A E E U C K S S C Y W U L Q L A
I R I R Q G M N S A C H G H D O S F G M
D V B A C K O F T H E N E T Z P X B N A
```

Back of the Net	Diving Header	Half Volley	Offside Rule
Big Game Player	Dugout	Hat-trick	One Touch
Brace	Dummy Run	Keepie Uppie	Playmaker
Class Act	Final Whistle	Man of the Match	Scissor Kick
Derby Day	Game of Two Halves	Mexican Wave	Screamer

PLAYER
OF THE SEASON

Following an outstanding 2022/23 campaign in the Seagulls' midfield, Ecuadorian international Moises Caicedo was named the club's Player of the Season having made 43 appearances in all competitions in what was Brighton & Hove Albion's greatest-ever season.

The all-action 21-year-old midfielder, now with Chelsea, enjoyed a double celebration at the club's annual awards presentation as not only did the fans vote him the Player of the Season, but his teammates backed up the supporters' verdict with Caicedo also confirmed as the Players' Player of the Season too.

Throughout the campaign, Caicedo was a star performer whose energetic box-to-box displays won him many plaudits. His consistent and impressive form for the Seagulls saw him included in the Ecuador squad for the 2022 FIFA World Cup finals in Qatar where the Albion man was on target in his country's final group match against Senegal.

After collecting the Player of the Season award and thanking the Albion fans who voted for him, he dedicated his award to his parents.

"When I go back to my flat I will give this award to my mother and father, they are my inspiration"

YOUNG PLAYER
OF THE SEASON

Teenage striker Evan Ferguson capped off a tremendous breakthrough season by ending the 2022/23 campaign with ten first-team goals and the club's coveted Young Player of the Season award.

Last season also saw the Bettystown-born striker make his full international debut for the Republic of Ireland. His first cap saw him make a late substitute appearance against Norway in November 2022. Then in March 2023 he marked his first international start with a goal against Latvia at the Aviva Stadium in Dublin.

On the back of an incredible 2022/23 season, even greater things are expected from this exciting young talent in the new season with Albion competing on both the domestic and European stage.

EVAN FERGUSON

MOISES CAICEDO

TOP CLASS PLAYERS NOT ONLY NEED TO WIN THE BALL IN MIDFIELD, BUT ALSO PROVIDE THAT CUTTING EDGE WHEN NEEDED TO BE ABLE TO PLAY THROUGH DEFENCES WITH QUICK, INCISIVE PASSING.

THE WALL PASS

With teams being very organised in modern football, it can be very difficult to break them down and create scoring opportunities. One of the best ways to achieve this is by using the 'wall pass', otherwise known as the quick one-two.

EXERCISE

In a non-pressurised situation, involving four players, A carries the ball forward towards a static defender (in this case a cone) and before reaching the defender, plays the ball to B before running around the opposite side to receive the one-touch return pass. A then delivers the ball safely to C who then repeats the exercise returning the ball to D, and in this way the exercise continues. Eventually a defender can be used to make the exercise more challenging, with all players being rotated every few minutes.

The exercise can progress into a five-a-side game, the diagram below shows how additional players (W) on the touchline can be used as 'walls' with just one touch available to help the man in possession of the ball.

Each touchline player can move up and down the touchline, but not enter the pitch - they can also play for either team.

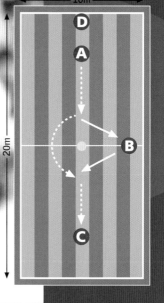

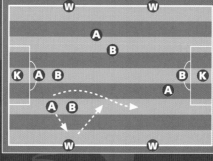

KEY FACTORS

1. Look to commit the defender before passing - do not play the ball too early.
2. Pass the ball firmly and to feet.
3. Accelerate past defender after passing.
4. Receiver (B) make themselves available for the pass.
5. B delivers a return pass, weighted correctly, into space.

SOCCER SKILLS

If done correctly, this is a tactic which is extremely difficult to stop, but needs teamwork and communication between the two attacking players.

JAMES
MILNER

A-Z

ARE YOU READY TO TACKLE OUR A-Z FOOTBALL QUIZ?

THE SIMPLE RULE IS THAT THE ANSWERS RUN THROUGH THE 26 LETTERS OF THE ALPHABET.

A
What nationality is Watford goalkeeper Daniel Bachmann?

A

B
Which team won the Sky Bet Championship title in 2022/23?

B

C
Which Premier League club reappointed their former manager as interim boss in March 2023?

C

D
Which League One side play their home matches at Pride Park?

D

E
What nationality is Liverpool's sensational striker Mohamed Salah?

E

F
Which country knocked England out of the FIFA World Cup finals in 2022?

F

34

G

Which famous football ground is due to host its final fixture in 2024?

G

 K

What is the name of Premier League new boys Luton Town's home ground?

K

L

Can you name the Ipswich Town striker who netted 17 League One goals in the Tractor Boys' 2022/23 promotion-winning season?

L

 M

Which Championship club boasted the division's top scorer in 2022/23?

M

H

Which club did Neil Warnock lead to Championship survival in 2022/23?

H

I

Which country did England defeat 6-2 in their opening game of the FIFA 2022 World Cup finals?

I

J

Aston Villa winger Leon Bailey plays internationally for which country?

J

ANSWERS ON PAGE 62

Q Can you name the country that hosted the FIFA 2022 World Cup finals?

Q

R Which Spanish side did Manchester City defeat in last season's UEFA Champions League semi-final?

R

S Which team knocked Premier League champions Manchester City out of the Carabao Cup last season?

S

N What nationality is Manchester City's ace marksman Erling Haaland?

N

T Which full-back left Huddersfield Town to join Nottingham Forest ahead of their return to the Premier League in the summer of 2022?

T

O Can you name the former Premier League team that will compete in the National League in 2023/24?

O

P Which international striker ended five seasons with Norwich City in May 2023?

P

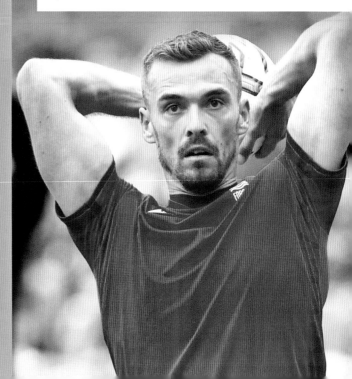

 X Can you name the Portuguese international defender who played in the Premier League with Everton, Liverpool & Middlesbrough?

 X

U Can you name Brighton's German forward who joined the Seagulls in January 2022?

U

 Y At which club did Leeds United's Luke Ayling make his league debut?

 Y

V Can you name the former England striker who has hit over 100 Premier League goals for Leicester City?

V

Z Which Dutch international midfielder played Premier League football for Chelsea, Middlesbrough and Liverpool in the 2000s?

Z

W Can you name the goalkeeper who got his name on the scoresheet last season in a Championship fixture?

W

A-Z

PART TWO

ANSWERS ON PAGE 62 37

DANNY
WELBECK
18

DESIGN A
FOOTY BOOT

Design a brilliant new footy boot
for the Seagulls squad!

MIDFIELD
MAESTROS

JIMMY CASE, ELLIOTT BENNETT AND ANTHONY KNOCKAERT ALL PROVIDED A CREATIVE AND GOALSCORING PRESENCE IN THE SEAGULLS' MIDFIELD. CONTINUING THAT FINE TRADITION IS BRIGHTON'S GERMAN MIDFIELD STAR PASCAL GROSS.

Elliott Bennett was an extremely popular member of the Seagulls' 2010/11 League One title-winning squad that secured Albion's promotion to the Championship.

Signed from Wolverhampton Wanderers in August 2009, Bennett was a hard-working creative presence on the right side of the Brighton midfield. Capable of scoring goals and setting up opportunities for others, Bennett's performances at Withdean Stadium won him many admirers and a place in the PFA League One Team of the Year for 2010/11.

He moved on to Norwich City in the summer of 2011 and starred for the Canaries at Premier League level before making a brief return to Albion on loan in 2014.

Jimmy Case might well be one to ask your parents about having been a real midfield powerhouse for Albion back in the early 1980s.

Recruited from Liverpool ahead of the 1981/82 First Division campaign, Case proved to be the inspirational driving force behind Brighton's memorable run to the 1983 FA Cup Final at Wembley. He netted vital goals in the matches away to Liverpool, at home to Norwich City and in the semi-final victory over Sheffield Wednesday.

A firm favourite in the Goldstone Ground days, Case took in a second spell with Albion when he became player/coach in 1993. He later served as manager too.

JIMMY CASE

DATE OF BIRTH: 18 May 1954

PLACE OF BIRTH: Liverpool

NATIONALITY: English

ALBION APPEARANCES: 183

ALBION GOALS: 15

ALBION DEBUT: 29 August 1981
West Ham United 1 Brighton & Hove Albion 1 (First Division)

ELLIOTT BENNETT

DATE OF BIRTH: 18 December 1988

PLACE OF BIRTH: Telford

NATIONALITY: English

ALBION APPEARANCES: 107

ALBION GOALS: 17

ALBION DEBUT: 22 August 2009
Brighton & Hove Albion 2 Stockport County 4 (League One)

Anthony Knockaert was a goalscoring winger who joined the Seagulls in 2016 from Belgian club Standard Liege.

After the setback of a promotion near-miss the previous season, Knockaert proved to be the real on-pitch driving force behind Albion's 2016/17 promotion-winning campaign. In scintillating form throughout the season, Knockaert's 15 Championship goals and numerous assists saw him voted the EFL Championship Player of the Season.

He was also named Brighton's Player of the Season at the conclusion of a memorable campaign that had seen the club return to the top flight for the first time 34 years. The 2017/18 season saw him feature in 33 Premier League games where his performances helped the Seagulls secure a 15th-place finish.

ANTHONY KNOCKAERT

DATE OF BIRTH:	20 November 1991
PLACE OF BIRTH:	Roubaix, France
NATIONALITY:	French
ALBION APPEARANCES:	139
ALBION GOALS:	27
ALBION DEBUT:	12 January 2016

Rotherham United 2 Brighton & Hove Albion 0 (Championship)

PASCAL GROSS

DATE OF BIRTH:	15 June 1991
PLACE OF BIRTH:	Mannheim, Germany
NATIONALITY:	German
ALBION APPEARANCES:	214*
ALBION GOALS:	27*
ALBION DEBUT:	12 August 2017

Brighton & Hove Albion 0 Manchester City 2 (Premier League)

*AS AT THE END OF THE 2022/23 SEASON

Pascal Gross etched his name into Brighton & Hove Albion folklore by scoring the club's first-ever Premier League goal as the Seagulls defeated West Bromwich Albion 3-1 at the Amex in September 2017.

The all-action German midfielder joined Albion from FC Ingolstadt in May 2017 ahead of the club's historic debut Premier League campaign. A consistent performer and one of the first names on the Albion teamsheet throughout his time at the club, 32-year-old Gross has now amassed over 200 appearances for Albion.

With the ability to operate in a number of midfield roles, a reward for his consistency was a debut appearance for Germany against Japan in September.

CLASSIC

Gully is hiding in five different places as Seagulls fans celebrate winning the League One Championship at Withdean Stadium in 2011.

FAN'TASTIC

Can you find all five?

ANSWERS ON PAGE 62

22 KAORU MITOMA

JULIO
ENCISO

GOAL

OF THE SEASON

The goal was the Paraguayan international's fourth Premier League strike of the season and proved enough to earn Roberto De Zerbi's side the point they needed to secure Europa League football at the Amex Stadium in 2023/24.

The teenager's previous three Albion goals had all arrived in away fixtures, but what a way to bag your first goal on home soil!

While Enciso's goal was the overwhelming choice for Goal of the Season, Kaoru Mitoma's brilliant last-gasp effort in the 2-1 FA Cup victory over Liverpool in January was runner-up.

Julio Enciso capped off an excellent debut campaign with the Seagulls by netting the club's Goal of the Season for 2022/23.

Arriving in the final home match of an historic Brighton & Hove Albion campaign, Enciso's stunning strike against treble-chasing Manchester City at the Amex in May was both sensational and vitally important.

Trailing to Phil Foden's 25th-minute opener for the champions, Enciso sparked wild scenes of delight among the home crowd seven minutes before the break when he drew the Seagulls level in style. The exciting forward let fly with a truly remarkable shot which arrowed into the top corner of the net from all of 25 yards out and left visiting City 'keeper Stefan Ortega helpless.

JULIO ENCISO

V MANCHESTER CITY

BEHIND THE

BADGE

... HIDDEN BEHIND OUR BEAUTIFUL BADGE?

A

B

C

48

F

G

D

E

H

49

JOÃO PEDRO

TRUE
COLOURS

**HAVE FUN COLOURING IN THIS
PICTURE OF SEAGULLS STAR
JOÃO PEDRO**

STUNNING STRIKERS

BOBBY ZAMORA, LEO ULLOA AND GLENN MURRAY WERE ALL ACE ALBION MARKSMEN. LOOKING TO FOLLOW IN THEIR FOOTSTEPS IS EXCITING REPUBLIC OF IRELAND STRIKER EVAN FERGUSON.

Leo Ulloa enjoyed an exceptional 18 months with Brighton between January 2013 and the summer of 2014 when he was transferred to then-Premier League Leicester City.

In a short but highly successful Albion career the Argentinean striker boasted an impressive goals-to-games ratio as he netted 26 times in just 58 appearances for the Seagulls.

A strong, powerful and mobile striker, Ulloa was the first Albion player to score at hat-trick at the Amex Stadium when he netted a treble in the 4-1 victory over Huddersfield Town in March 2013. He gained further legendary status with the Albion fans later that month when he scored twice in a 3-0 victory over arch-rivals Crystal Palace.

Bobby Zamora is a Brighton goalscoring legend who enjoyed two spells with the club and his £100,000 signing from Bristol Rovers in 2000 remains one of the club's smartest pieces of transfer business.

During his first full season he netted an incredible 31 goals in all competitions as Brighton won the Third Division title in 2000/01. His 32 goals the following season proved to be vital as Albion achieved back-to-back promotions when they landed the 2001/02 Second Division title.

After leaving the Seagulls in 2003 for Premier League Tottenham Hotspur, Zamora made an emotional return to Brighton for the 2015/16 campaign and helped Albion reach the Championship Play-Offs.

BOBBY ZAMORA

DATE OF BIRTH: 16 January 1981

PLACE OF BIRTH: Barking

NATIONALITY: English

ALBION APPEARANCES: 152

ALBION GOALS: 90

ALBION DEBUT: 12 February 2000
Brighton & Hove Albion 1 Plymouth Argyle 1 (Division Three)

LEO ULLOA

DATE OF BIRTH: 26 July 1986

PLACE OF BIRTH: General Roca, Argentina

NATIONALITY: Argentinean

ALBION APPEARANCES: 58

ALBION GOALS: 26

ALBION DEBUT: 26 January 2013
Brighton & Hove Albion 2 Arsenal 3 (FA Cup)

Glenn Murray riffled home a superb 111 goals for the Seagulls in 287 appearances and sits second in the club's list of all-time goalscorers.

Like many Albion greats, Murray enjoyed two spells with the club and plied his trade for the Seagulls at both Withdean Stadium and the Amex.

Initially joining from Rochdale in January 2008, he marked his home debut with a brace against Crewe Alexandra and proceeded to net goals in Albion colours in League One, the Championship and the Premier League. A real hardworking striker who never gave opposing defenders a moment of peace, Murray developed cult status with the Brighton fans.

GLENN MURRAY

DATE OF BIRTH: 25 September 1983

PLACE OF BIRTH: Barrow

NATIONALITY: English

ALBION APPEARANCES: 287

ALBION GOALS: 111

ALBION DEBUT: 29 January 2008
Northampton Town 1 Brighton & Hove Albion 0 (League One)

EVAN FERGUSON

DATE OF BIRTH: 19 October 2004

PLACE OF BIRTH: Bettystown, Ireland

NATIONALITY: Irish

ALBION APPEARANCES: 29*

ALBION GOALS: 10*

ALBION DEBUT: 24 August 2021
Cardiff City 0 Brighton & Hove Albion 1 (League Cup)

*AS AT THE END OF THE 2022/23 SEASON

Evan Ferguson is an exceptionally talented teenager whose name is on the lips of every supporter at the Amex Stadium. The Republic of Ireland international certainly appears to have a great future ahead of him having made a superb impression on the Albion first team last season.

Ferguson capped off a tremendous breakthrough season by ending the 2022/23 campaign with ten first-team goals and winning Albion's prestigious Young Player of the Season award.

Already a goalscorer at full international level for the Republic, great things are expected from this exciting young talent in the 2023/24 season after he netted four goals in his opening four games of the campaign.

REWIND

THREE GREAT SEAGULLS VICTORIES FROM 2023

Brighton & Hove Albion 6
Wolverhampton Wanderers 0

PREMIER LEAGUE · APRIL 29, 2023

Albion registered their most comprehensive Premier League victory to date as Roberto De Zerbi's men turned on the style when they fired six goals past Wolves without reply.

Deniz Undav began the rout when he opened the scoring after just six minutes and that early goal certainly set the tone for what was to follow. The hosts had racked-up a four-goal lead by half-time thanks to a brace from Pascal Gross and Danny Welbeck's sixth goal of the season.

Welbeck and Undav both took their afternoon's tally to two with second-half goals as Albion bounced back from a surprise defeat to Nott'm Forest in their previous fixture in the best possible manner.

Brighton & Hove Albion 1
Manchester United 0

PREMIER LEAGUE · MAY 4, 2023

A last-gasp Alexis Mac Allister penalty gave the Seagulls sweet revenge over Manchester United having suffered an FA Cup semi-final penalty shootout defeat to the Red Devils at Wembley just three matches earlier.

After United defender Luke Shaw had handled in the area, Mac Allister kept his cool from the spot to rifle home the game's only goal with 99 minutes on the clock.

The late winner was met with a crescendo of noise from the Amex crowd and gave Brighton a first ever league double over Manchester United.

Arsenal 0
Brighton & Hove Albion 3

PREMIER LEAGUE · MAY 14, 2023

Arsenal's slim hopes of landing the Premier League title for 2022/23 were dealt a hammer blow by an outstanding away performance from the Seagulls.

This win gave Albion's bid for European football a major boost at the team pressed on search of a best-ever league finish. An exciting match saw former Albion man Leandro Trossard hit the crossbar for the Gunners before Julio Enciso's header gave Brighton a 51st-minute lead. Deniz Undav then lobbed home 'keeper Aaron Ramsdale four minutes from time to double the Seagulls' advantage and Pervis Estupiñán wrapped up the win with Albion's third in injury time.

FAST FORWARD

Crystal Palace (HOME)

PREMIER LEAGUE · FEBRUARY 3, 2024

After Solly March netted the only goal of the game to give the Seagulls victory over arch-rivals Crystal Palace at the Amex in March 2023, Brighton will be aiming for a second consecutive victory over the Eagles on home soil.

Under the management of the vastly experienced Roy Hodgson, Palace are sure to be a well-drilled and tough opponent but Roberto De Zerbi's team fear no-one at the Amex and will be looking to give their supporters the derby bragging rights once again.

With a win and a draw against their rivals last season, Albion will be looking to go one better in 2023/24 with a Premier League double over Palace for the first time since 2018/19.

Manchester City (HOME)

PREMIER LEAGUE · MARCH 16, 2024

Brighton will welcome treble-winning Manchester City to the Amex in March for what will certainly be one of the toughest home assignments of the season for the Seagulls.

Every player loves nothing more than testing themselves against the best and Pep Guardiola's team certainly are just that right now. Keeping tabs on the goalscoring talents of Erling Haaland will be just one of many challenges facing Albion in a match where every player will need to be on their game.

Albion will certainly draw great confidence from the 1-1 draw between the two sides at the Amex at the end of last season, where Julio Enciso's 38th-minute goal cancelled out Phil Foden's 25th-minute opener for all-conquering City.

Manchester United (HOME)

PREMIER LEAGUE · MAY 19, 2024

Albion's 2023/24 Premier League campaign concludes with a visit from 2022/23 League Cup winners Manchester United.

The Seagulls enjoyed a first league double over the Old Trafford club last season and have certainly had some memorable victories over the Red Devils since winning promotion to the Premier League back in 2017.

Pascal Gross' historic winner over United here in May 2018 certainly set the tone for some classic clashes with the red side of Manchester. The Amex has witnessed a 3-2 home win in August 2018, a sensational 4-0 Albion victory in May 2022 and last season's dramatic late winning penalty. If what has gone before is anything to go by, then the final game of the season could well be a cracker.

BEING PREDICTABLE IS EASY IN FOOTBALL.

DOING THE UNEXPECTED IS A LOT MORE DIFFICULT.

TURNING
WITH
THE BALL

One of the biggest problems a defence can have to deal with is when a skilful player is prepared to turn with the ball and run at them, committing a key defender into making a challenge. Because football today is so fast and space so precious, this is becoming a rare skill.

EXERCISE 1

In an area 20m x 10m, A plays the ball into B who turns, and with two touches maximum plays the ball into C. C controls and reverses the process. After a few minutes the middleman is changed.

As you progress, a defender is brought in to oppose B, and is initially encouraged to play a 'passive' role. B has to turn and play the ball to C who is allowed to move along the baseline.

The type of turns can vary. Players should be encouraged to use the outside of the foot, inside of the foot, with feint and disguise to make space for the turn.

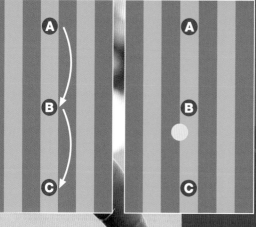

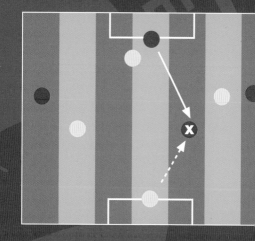

EXERCISE 2

As the players grow in confidence, you can move forward to a small-sided game. In this example of a 4-a-side practice match, X has made space for himself to turn with the ball, by coming off his defender at an angle. By doing this he can see that the defender has not tracked him, and therefore has the awareness to turn and attack.

SOCCER
SKILLS

Matches at the top level are won and lost by pieces of skill such as this, so players have to be brave enough to go in search of the ball, and turn in tight situations.

BRIGHTON & HOVE ALBION

30 PERVIS ESTUPIÑÁN

HIGH
FIVES

TEST YOUR ALBION KNOWLEDGE & MEMORY WITH OUR HIGH FIVES QUIZ

1. Across the previous five seasons, who have been Albion's leading league goalscorers?

1.
2.
3.
4.
5.

2. Can you name Brighton's last five FA Cup opponents ahead of the 2023/24 season?

1.
2.
3.
4.
5.

3. Prior to Roberto De Zerbi, who were the Seagulls' last five permanent managers?

1.
2.
3.
4.
5.

4. Name Albion's last five EFL Cup opponents as at the end of the 2022/23 season?

1.
2.
3.
4.
5.

5. Can you remember the Seagulls' final league position from each of the last five seasons?

1. _____

2. _____

3. _____

4. _____

5. _____

8. Can you recall the score and season from our last five wins over rivals Crystal Palace?

1. _____

2. _____

3. _____

4. _____

5. _____

6. Which members of the Brighton squad started the most league games last season?

1. _____

2. _____

3. _____

4. _____

5. _____

9. Can you remember the Seagulls' last five Premier League victories from last season?

1. _____

2. _____

3. _____

4. _____

5. _____

7. Can you recall these players' Premier League squad numbers from 2022/23?

1. Julio Enciso

2. Evan Ferguson

3. Lewis Dunk

4. Adam Lallana

5. Billy Gillmour

10. Can you recall the club's end of season points tally from the last five seasons?

1. _____

2. _____

3. _____

4. _____

5. _____

ANSWERS ON PAGE 62

SENSATIONAL
STOPPERS

TOMASZ KUSZCZAK, DAVID STOCKDALE AND MATHEW RYAN WERE ALL GREAT ALBION 'KEEPERS. CONTINUING THAT PROUD TREND IS CURRENT SEAGULLS STOPPER JASON STEELE.

David Stockdale was an outstanding performer during the club's memorable 2016/17 promotion-winning season as Chris Hughton's side brought Premier League football to Brighton.

Signed from Fulham in the summer of 2014, Stockdale soon made the Albion No.1 shirt his own and kept 17 cleansheets in 2015/16 as Albion ended the season in third spot before succumbing to Sheffield Wednesday in the Play-Offs.

His assured performances really provided confidence to those playing in front of him and in 2016/17 he was in arguably the best form of his career and kept an exceptional 20 shutouts during the promotion-winning campaign.

Tomasz Kuszczak played a vital role as Albion emerged as serious promotion contenders from the Championship in 2012/13 and again in 2013/14.

Signed from Manchester United, the Poland international goalkeeper arrived at the Amex Stadium in June 2012 having impressed in loan spells with both West Bromwich Albion and Watford. In each of his two seasons with the Seagulls the club reached the Championship Play-Offs, but frustratingly were unable to push on and secure promotion.

Blessed with excellent positional sense and first-class reflexes, Kuszczak pulled off a vast number of eye-catching and important saves during his time at Brighton.

TOMASZ KUSZCZAK

DATE OF BIRTH: 20 March 1982

PLACE OF BIRTH: Krosno Odrzańskie, Poland

NATIONALITY: Polish

ALBION APPEARANCES: 89

ALBION DEBUT: 14th August 2012
Swindon Town 3 Brighton & Hove Albion 0 (League Cup)

DAVID STOCKDALE

DATE OF BIRTH: 20 September 1985

PLACE OF BIRTH: Leeds

NATIONALITY: English

ALBION APPEARANCES: 139

ALBION DEBUT: 9 August 2014
Brighton & Hove Albion 0 Sheffield Wednesday 1 (Championship

Mathew Ryan joined the Seagulls ahead of their first Premier League adventure in 2017/18.

The Australian stopper agreed a five-year deal with Albion in June 2017 when he arrived from Valencia and his signing proved an inspired move by then-Albion boss Chris Hughton. Across the next three-and-a-half seasons, the goalkeeper became a model of consistency as Albion survived and prospered in the Premier League.

A commanding character with the ability to take full control of his penalty area, Ryan proved to be a great shot-stopper and a highly reliable last line of defence. At international level his career has also seen him win over 0 full caps for the Socceroos.

MATHEW RYAN

DATE OF BIRTH: 8 April 1992

PLACE OF BIRTH: New South Wales, Australia

NATIONALITY: Australian

ALBION APPEARANCES: 123

ALBION DEBUT: 12 August 2017
Brighton & Hove Albion 0 Manchester City 2 (Premier League)

JASON STEELE

DATE OF BIRTH: 18 August 1990

PLACE OF BIRTH: Newton Aycliffe

NATIONALITY: English

ALBION APPEARANCES: 30*

ALBION DEBUT: 5 January 2019
AFC Bournemouth 1 Brighton & Hove Albion 3 (FA Cup)

*AS AT THE END OF THE 2022/23 SEASON

Jason Steele had to be patient in his pursuit of first-team football at the Amex, but once handed the opportunity by Roberto De Zerbi in the second half of the 2022/23 campaign he certainly showed his worth.

An experienced goalkeeper, 33-year-old Steele joined Albion in June 2018 from Sunderland, having begun his career with Middlesbrough. He has also taken in spells with Blackburn Rovers and Northampton Town (loan).

A former England under-21 international, Steele also represented his country at the London 2012 Olympics and played a key role in helping to bring European football to Sussex for 2023/24.

ANSWERS

PAGE 29: FOOTY PHRASES

Keepie Uppie.

PAGE 34: A-Z QUIZ

A. Austrian. B. Burnley. C. Crystal Palace. D. Derby County. E. Egyptian.
F. France. G. Goodison Park (Everton). H. Huddersfield Town. I. Iran.
J. Jamaica. K. Kenilworth Road. L. Ladapo, Freddie. M. Middlesbrough
(Chuba Akpom). N. Norwegian. O. Oldham Athletic. P. Pukki, Teemu.
Q. Qatar. R. Real Madrid. S. Southampton. T. Toffolo, Harry. U. Undav,
Deniz. V. Vardy, Jamie. W. Wilson, Ben (Coventry City). X. Xavier, Abel.
Y. Yeovil Town. Z. Zenden, Boudewijn.

PAGE 42: FAN'TASTIC

PAGE 48: BEHIND THE BADGE

A. Evan Ferguson. B. Kaoru Mitoma.
C. Kaoru Mitoma. D. Danny Welbeck.
E. James Milner. F. Solly March.
G. Julio Enciso. H. Solly March.

PAGE 58: HIGH FIVES

QUIZ 1: 1. 2022/23, Alexis Mac Allister
(10 goals). 2. 2021/23, Leandro Trossard
& Neal Maupay (8 goals each).
3. 2020/21, Neal Maupay (8 goals).
4. 2019/20, Neal Maupay (10 goals).
5. 2018/19, Glenn Murray (13 goals).

QUIZ 2: 1. 2022/23, Manchester United
(semi-final). 2. 2022/23, Grimsby Town
(quarter-final). 3. 2022/23, Stoke City
(fifth round). 4. 2022/23, Liverpool (fourth round).
5. 2022/23, Middlesbrough (third round).

QUIZ 3: 1. Graham Potter. 2. Chris Hughton. 3. Sami Hyypia.
4. Oscar Garcia. 5. Gus Poyet.

QUIZ 4: 1. Charlton Athletic (2022/23). 2. Arsenal (2022/23).
3. Forest Green (2022/23). 4. Leicester City (2021/22).
5. Swansea City (2020/21).

QUIZ 5: 1. 6th in Premier League (2022/23). 2. 9th in Premier League
(2021/22). 3. 16th in Premier League (2020/21). 4. 15th in Premier
League (2019/20). 5. 17th in Premier League (2018/19).

QUIZ 6: 1. Pascal Gross (37 Premier League starts).
2. Lewis Dunk (36 Premier League starts).
3. Moises Caicedo (34 Premier League starts).
4. Alexis Mac Allister (31 Premier League starts).
5. Pervis Estupinan (31 Premier League starts).

QUIZ 7: 1. 20. 2. 28. 3. 5. 4. 14. 5. 27

QUIZ 8: 1. 2021/22, Brighton 1 Palace 0 (Premier League).
2. 2018/19, Palace 1-2 Brighton (Premier League).
3. 2018/19, Brighton 3-1 Palace (Premier League).
4. 2017/18, Brighton 2-1 Palace (FA Cup).
5. 2012/13, Brighton 3-0 Palace (Championship) .

QUIZ 9: 1. Brighton 3-1 Southampton. 2. Arsenal 0-3 Brighton.
3. Brighton 1-0 Manchester United. 4. Brighton 6-0 Wolverhampton
Wanderers. 5. Chelsea 1-2 Brighton.

QUIZ 10: 1. 2022/23, 62 points. 2. 2021/22, 51 points.
3. 2020/21, 41 points. 4. 2019/20, 41 points. 5. 2018/19, 36 points.

CLASSIC

FAN'TASTIC

Can you find all five?